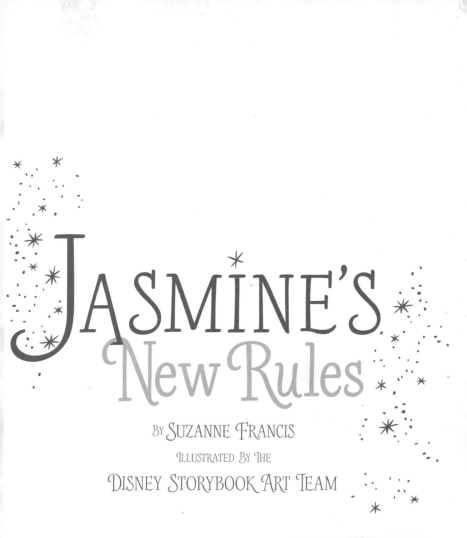

JASMINE'S
New Rules

By Suzanne Francis

Illustrated By The

Disney Storybook Art Team

Autumn
Publishing

For Al Francis,

who I am so fortunate to call my father

—S.F.

Published in 2019
by Autumn Publishing
Cottage Farm
Sywell
NN6 0BJ
www.igloobooks.com

Written by Suzanne Francis
Illustrated by Disney Storybook Art Team

GRA005 0119
2 4 6 8 10 9 7 5 3 1
ISBN 978-1-78905-530-6

Printed and manufactured in Italy

Chapter 1
Sunny Days

Jasmine gazed out the library window. As the sun shone down on the palace grounds, everything from the fountains to the flowers shimmered, giving off a jewel-like sparkle. She couldn't take her eyes off the view and longed to go outside and play.

Two snowy-white doves splashed around in one of the fountains below, and Jasmine watched, mesmerised, as beads of water flew off their feathers and disappeared into the grass.

Rajah, her tiger cub, was lazily stretched out on the warm patio. He rolled over onto his back and gazed up at her. Jasmine wanted to join him out in the sun. She had been trying to teach him how to play hide-and-seek, and he seemed close to getting it. Just the other day, she was certain that he'd actually tried to hide when she'd found him behind the giant date tree.

"Jasmine, please focus!" A sharp, cutting voice broke her from her trance. Jasmine's teacher, Miss Leila, normally spoke very softly, but when she was angry her voice became shrill. The sound startled Jasmine and brought her attention back inside the library.

Miss Leila returned to her soft voice. "You should be practising your writing, not daydreaming."

Jasmine, who often said exactly what she was thinking, replied, "But it's the perfect day to be playing outside." She knew she couldn't be blamed for lacking focus. After all, sunny days were meant to be spent outdoors.

However, Miss Leila wore a frustrated

expression. Her thick, dark eyebrows were arched into peaks that nearly touched her hairline. "You must finish this – and make sure to finish it well – before you go outside," she said.

Jasmine nodded. She dipped her stylus into the inkwell, then touched it to her paper,  writing the intricate script letters of the alphabet. Each curve and dot was a struggle. She felt the urge to finish her work quickly, but she knew if she made a mistake, Miss Leila would force her to begin again.

So she did her best to concentrate. Once she was done, she waited patiently for Miss Leila to approve her work.

"Very good," Miss Leila said, looking at Jasmine's writing. "This afternoon—"

Without thinking, Jasmine got up from her seat and moved towards the door, ready to dash out. But Miss Leila stopped her by clearing her throat and saying, "It is not proper to walk away when someone is speaking to you." Miss Leila raised her eyebrows again as Jasmine faced her and waited. The teacher took a deep breath before continuing. "Later today, after you meet with your father, we will work on reading. Now you may be excused from your lesson."

Jasmine bowed her head in gratitude and smiled. "Thank you, Miss Leila," she said. Finally she could play outside!

She rushed out of the library and picked up speed as she ran down the hall and through the palace door. Rajah pranced over to greet her, rubbing his body against her leg. "Hello, Rajah," said Jasmine, petting his head. "Are you ready?" The tiger cub looked up at her eagerly, and Jasmine smiled. "Let's run!" she cried, taking off towards the rose garden. Rajah raced after her and quickly caught up. The two ran alongside each other across the grounds and over to a beautiful arched entrance.

As she caught her breath, Jasmine admired the cream-coloured roses that scrambled up and over the arch. She leant forwards and put her face in one of the beautiful flowers, inhaling deeply and enjoying the sweet scent. Rajah leant in to smell one too and a bee buzzed near his nose, surprising him. He shook his head and let out a little growl.

Jasmine laughed. "You're all right," she said, examining him. "Now, do you remember what I taught you?" she asked,

bringing his soft face up to hers. "I'll count and you hide."

Jasmine got up and turned round. She put her hands over her eyes and started to count. But she could feel that Rajah hadn't moved. She turned back to peek through her fingers and saw him sitting, looking up at her curiously. "You hide," she repeated. "Go ahead. Go hide." She motioned to a bed of pink roses that lined the high wall surrounding the grounds. Rajah trotted over to them. Jasmine quickly put her hands in front of her face and began to count again.

"… eight… nine… ten!" she shouted. She removed her hands from her face and saw Rajah still sitting by the pink rose bush licking his fur. She smiled and ran over to the cub. "Very good," she said, gently scratching behind his ears. "I think you're getting better."

Just then she heard a chorus of laughter and squeals coming from the other side of the wall. It was a group of children running around and playing together. She tried jumping up to catch a glimpse, but the wall was too high. She sat down and leant against the warm stucco, listening. Closing her eyes, she imagined that she was out there with them, playing and having fun.

"Jasmine!" Miss Leila's loud, high-pitched

voice rang out, calling her back in. As Miss Leila approached, Jasmine's eyes opened. "Why are you sitting in the rose bed?" her teacher asked. "You're getting your clothes dirty."

Jasmine looked down. She hadn't even noticed where she was sitting, but it was true – there were spots of dark soil on her light-blue trousers. She stood up and brushed the dirt away. "I was listening to the children. I wish I could go play with them," she said, looking at Miss Leila with hopeful eyes.

"You know you must stay in the palace

grounds," said Miss Leila, helping Jasmine get the dirt off her trousers. "And besides, it would be completely improper for you to play with anyone who isn't royalty."

The princess looked down at the ground. She knew those were the rules, but she didn't like them. Rajah nuzzled Jasmine's hand, begging for a scratch. She obliged, and he gave her a grateful lick.

"Come now," said Miss Leila, gently. "It's time for your tea. Your father is waiting."

Jasmine, with Rajah by her side, followed her teacher back into the palace.

Chapter 2
An Old Friend

The Sultan's eyes twinkled and his mouth turned up in a bright, jolly grin as soon as he saw Princess Jasmine enter the room. "Hello, my dear," he said. "I'm so very pleased that my favourite time of the day has come. A well-deserved break for me and my daughter. How is your day going?"

Jasmine told him about her morning as they were served tea, fruit and pastries.

Then, she cautiously mentioned the children she'd heard playing outside the palace walls. "I couldn't see them, but I could tell they were having a lot of fun. And I wanted to play with them and have fun, too." She didn't look up at her father while she waited for his response.

"Jasmine, you are a princess. And you may not leave the palace grounds," the Sultan said.

"I know, Father, but maybe we could open the gates and invite them in," she suggested. "Then I wouldn't be leaving and we could play together here."

"Oh, dear. That would not be proper.

You are only supposed to play with royal children."

"But—" Jasmine started.

"No, no," her father said, shaking his head. "It's just not the way things work. And it is not up for discussion." He bit into a sweet, flaky pastry stuffed with dried figs.

Jasmine sighed as she took a sip of her warm, spicy tea.

Suddenly, Armand, the Sultan's faithful servant, entered carrying a package. He brought it over to the Sultan. "What is it?" the Sultan asked, eyeing the package curiously.

"It just arrived. I thought you would want to open it right away," said Armand, a smile creeping across his face. "It is from Gazsi," he added in an excited hush.

The Sultan chuckled and eagerly reached for the package. "Gazsi? Of course. Thank you, thank you, Armand."

Even though Jasmine couldn't remember meeting Gazsi, she felt as if she knew him well. He had been a good friend of her father's since he was a boy, and she loved hearing stories about the things they had done together. The Sultan ripped open the package, eager to see what was inside.

"What is it?" Jasmine asked, intrigued.

The Sultan pulled out a square, flat piece of smooth wood covered in a pattern of dark brown and tan squares. "I don't know," he said, examining the strange object. He peered into the package and removed a small green velvet bag that was tied with a string.

Inside the bag were small carved stone figures. Jasmine quickly counted them – thirty-two in all. Half of them were dark brown and half were tan, like the squares on the wood. She spread them out across the table, divided them up by colour and put them into two separate piles, standing them on their flat side. Each

set had eight pieces that were the same size and shape. There were also several pairs of slightly bigger figures with tiny details that set them apart. Two pieces, one of each colour, had deep cuts at the top that looked a little like crowns.

The Sultan unfolded a note and began to read it.

"What is it, Father?" Jasmine asked.

"It's a game," said the Sultan. "Gazsi says it is called 'chess' and he will be here to challenge me in a few weeks." He laughed again, bubbling with happiness. "He and I haven't seen each other in a long time," the Sultan continued, examining the game and its pieces. "Oh, we used to have such fun together. Got into quite a bit of trouble, too. Nothing dangerous, of course," he added quickly.

"Tell me. Please," Jasmine begged. "Just one little story."

The Sultan leant back in his chair and grinned mischievously. "Let's see…" He looked at his daughter for a moment, as if deciding which tale to tell her. "One time, Gazsi and I were riding our horses, exploring the desert around his father's palace," he began. "We'd gone a bit farther that day than ever before. Just as we were about to turn back, we came upon an old stone tower."

Jasmine listened, fascinated, as her father told her about how he and Gazsi explored the mysterious tower. They discovered ancient symbols scratched into the walls and found an old box hidden behind one of the tower's stones.

"What was inside it?" Jasmine asked, leaning forwards.

The Sultan smiled, enjoying Jasmine's wide eyes as she waited in anticipation. He went into great detail about how he and Gazsi had gone back and forth, deciding

who would open the box. Finally, they each picked a palm-sized rock and agreed that whoever threw his rock farther would open the box. Gazsi was the victor, so he opened it.

"As Gazsi slowly prised open the old box, it made a creaking noise that told us it hadn't been open for thousands of years." Jasmine nodded enthusiastically, ready to finally hear about the contents of the box. The Sultan's eyes opened wide and his eyebrows danced up towards the top of his head. "Inside was a medallion with a strange hole cut out of the centre," he said in an excited hush. "We thought it might even be a key."

"To what?" asked Jasmine.

"We didn't know," said the Sultan, leaning back in his chair again. "But we had many adventures trying to find out."

"It sounds very mysterious."

"Yes, yes, it was," the Sultan said, eyeing the chessboard. "Now I shall take a look at this game. A new adventure! I must say I am very eager to begin."

The Sultan rubbed his hands together as he looked over the board. Jasmine picked up one of the pieces. The edges were smooth and cold. "I wonder how you play," she said, curious.

"We shall find out!" said the Sultan.

"Jasmine." Miss Leila's voice cut through the fun once again. "Time to get back to work."

The rest of the day went on like every other. After another few hours of reading, writing and mathematics, Jasmine ate dinner, took a bath and went to bed.

As she closed her eyes and tried to fall asleep, she couldn't help thinking about the story her father had told her about his adventure with Gazsi. How wonderful it all sounded! Maybe one day she would have a friend to explore the world with. Her mind began to spin, imagining the adventures that might be in her future.

She reached down and scratched Rajah's head, happy to have him as a companion. He purred beside her, and soon the two fell asleep.

Chapter 3
The Bet

The next morning, when Jasmine met her father for breakfast, the chess game was on the table. He had spent a good portion of the night learning how to play and was eager for an opponent. "Good morning, dear," he said, without looking up from the chessboard.

"So? How do you play?" Jasmine asked, admiring the game pieces her father had set out.

The Sultan began to explain what he had learnt. He told Jasmine that each piece had a special way of moving across the board. The object of the game was to use those moves to capture your opponent's king. Jasmine listened carefully and picked up the rules quickly. "Let's play," she said. "That will be the best way to learn."

"You are quite right," said the Sultan. He couldn't wait!

When Miss Leila entered to take Jasmine away for her lessons, the Sultan told her that Jasmine would be spending the day learning how to play chess. Jasmine was thrilled at the change of pace and the prospect of a whole day with her father.

The morning passed quickly as Jasmine and the Sultan concentrated on their game. They had to be reminded of lunchtime and took only a short break to eat before continuing.

The Sultan won the first game, but Jasmine immediately challenged him to another. He was very happy to accept.

"If I beat you, will you grant me a wish?" she asked.

"That sounds like a bet," said the Sultan, looking at his daughter through squinted eyes. She knew he loved a friendly competition.

Jasmine nodded. "It is." The Sultan thought for a moment. "Afraid you might lose?" Jasmine asked jokingly.

"A wish," the Sultan said with a chuckle. "Okay, but within reason," he added, accepting her proposal.

"Within reason," she repeated, nodding in agreement. Then, she smiled as she eyed the board and moved her first figure forwards two squares.

Jasmine watched her father consider his move. His fingers tapped the edge of the table as he examined the board. Finally, he moved one of his pieces forwards and Jasmine began planning what she should do next, soon realising that part of the game was thinking ahead.

After hours of playing, the Sultan took Jasmine's queen and she thought she might lose. But with her next few moves, she managed to get his queen. Before he could figure out her plan, Jasmine swooped in and captured the Sultan's king!

Despite losing, the Sultan couldn't help being delighted. He was proud of Jasmine. He was also eager for another game. Before

he could challenge his daughter to a rematch, though, she reminded him of the bet they'd made.

"So," she said with a sly smile. "About my wish…"

"Oh, yes," said the Sultan. "You won, so I must oblige. What is your request? Within reason, remember."

"Father, I want to play with someone my age," said Jasmine. "It's always just me and Rajah, and—"

"Yes, yes," said the Sultan. "Say no more. I understand. It has been quite some time since you've played with another child, hasn't it?" He scratched his chin, deep in thought.

"Gazsi has a son just about your age," he began. "I believe he is nine years old. His name is Kav. I will grant your wish and invite him to come along with his father on his visit."

Jasmine jumped up from her seat and threw her arms round her father's neck. "Oh, Father. Thank you!" she exclaimed.

The Sultan hugged her tightly. "But first," he said, releasing her, "let's play again. I must improve. I can't let that old Gazsi come here and beat me like my daughter." The

Sultan smiled and the two started another game. "But no more bets between you and me," he added with a grin. "We'll just play for the honour of winning or the lesson of losing."

Jasmine smiled as they put their pieces on the board. "Prepare for your lesson, Father."

The Sultan laughed at his daughter's bold attitude. "We shall see," he said.

Chapter 4

The Arrival

Over the next few weeks, Jasmine found it very difficult to focus on anything as she eagerly awaited Kav's arrival. Even the things she normally enjoyed seemed dull. The chef made her favourite almond pastries, but they didn't taste as delicious as usual. Visiting the stables and feeding apples to the horses felt like a chore rather than a treat. Even watching the pink flamingos wade in the pond and catch fish with their big black beaks was dreary. Normally she loved taking her evening bath, but instead of playing in the water, she found herself counting the small mosaic tiles on the ceiling, waiting for the time to pass.

The only thing that seemed to help was playing chess with her father. Their games got longer and longer as they both became better. But when she wasn't playing chess, she was thinking about Kav and wondering what he would be like and what fun they might have together. She imagined them playing and having adventures like her father and Gazsi, laughing and joking like the kids she'd heard on the other side of the palace wall. She simply couldn't wait to meet her new friend.

Then one morning Jasmine awoke to the sound of dozens of hooves clopping against the ground outside. She leapt out of bed and threw on her robe. Rajah pranced along, following as Jasmine hurried to her balcony. She looked over the edge and saw a thrilling sight below: Gazsi and Kav were stepping out of a great golden carriage led by a team of horses! Jasmine rushed back into her bedroom to get dressed before she and Rajah raced downstairs and out the front door.

"Gazsi," the Sultan said, as he stepped towards his friend for a hug.

Gazsi was a tall man with warm brown eyes and a pointed nose that bent towards his lips. "It is good to see you, old friend." He smiled widely at the Sultan. "And this must be Princess Jasmine." Gazsi turned towards the princess. "I have not seen you since you were this high," he said, holding his hand above the ground around his knee.

"It is so nice to see you, Gazsi," said Jasmine, suddenly feeling shy.

Gazsi beamed as he proudly introduced Kav, his son. Kav looked a lot like his father, but his eyes were jade green. And though he wore a straight face, his eyes were full of wonder as he looked up at Jasmine.

"Hello," he said softly.

The Sultan greeted Kav and then turned to Gazsi.

"Well?" said Gazsi, smiling at the Sultan. "What do you think?"

The Sultan grinned brightly and said, "I think you are about to lose at your own game."

Gazsi threw his hands in the air and laughed. "Aha! That's the spirit." Then, he patted the Sultan on the shoulder and added, "I cannot wait to beat you, my friend! I have missed you very much."

The Sultan and Gazsi laughed like young children. When they stopped, the Sultan asked, "And the stakes? The usual, I presume?"

Gazsi thought for a moment, then chuckled mischievously and said, "Yes. The usual."

"Wonderful," said the Sultan. "This will be quite a game."

Jasmine and Kav watched as their fathers walked away, wondering what stakes they could be talking about. But before they were able to ask questions, the two men hurried inside the palace to start their first game of chess.

"Have fun, you two," called the Sultan.

"Yes," added Gazsi, as they walked off. "Enjoy each other's company! Have an adventure!"

"But no adventure beyond the walls," the Sultan called back to Jasmine before he and Gazsi disappeared through the palace doors.

Kav and Jasmine looked at each other for a moment.

"I'm so happy you're here," said Jasmine, trying to make Kav feel comfortable and welcome. "What do you want to do?"

Kav shrugged and walked over to his bag.

"Want to play in the rose garden?" Jasmine asked eagerly. She couldn't wait to start having fun. "It's just over there." She pointed towards it.

Kav shook his head as he looked through his bag. "I think I'll practise," he said, pulling out a chessboard and a small pouch. "My father taught me how to play." He looked around, searching for a good place to set up the game.

"We could sit over there," said Jasmine, gesturing towards a table near a huge fig tree.

"Do you know the game?" Kav asked, as he followed her to the table.

Jasmine nodded. "My father taught me also. We've been playing a lot."

Kav put the board down and emptied the

contents of the pouch. Wooden game pieces spilt out. Unlike the stone figures in her father's set, these shapes were very distinct. The eight smallest pieces looked like soldiers. Then there were two castles, two horses and two bishops. The tallest pieces looked just like a king and a queen. They were beautiful.

Jasmine reached out to hold one of the dark-brown soldier pieces, but Kav swiped it. She frowned as she looked at him, surprised by his rude reaction.

"I'll be dark brown," he said. "You can be tan."

"All right," said Jasmine, picking up the tan pieces and placing them on the board.

As the two sat and started to play, Kav began to talk. Jasmine asked what his kingdom was like and he told her all about his palace. When she asked about the people and the food, he continued to ramble on about how big and fancy his home was. "It's the most amazing palace I've ever seen," said Kav, moving one of his soldiers, or pawns. "And I have seen many."

Jasmine knew that Kav and his father frequently travelled, so she asked him about that as she moved one of her pawns. "What was your favourite trip?"

"Egypt was interesting," said Kav.

Jasmine gasped with excitement. "I've read books about Egypt," she said. "I like Cleopatra."

"She was very rich," Kav said, moving another pawn.

"And very smart," added Jasmine. "Did you see the ancient pyramids?" she asked, contemplating her next move.

Kav nodded.

"What were they like?"

"They look like pyramids," Kav said, shrugging.

Jasmine moved another game piece diagonally, capturing one of Kav's pawns. "I would love to see them for myself. Maybe some day…"

Then, Kav moved one of his pawns to capture one of Jasmine's. "Our carriage is covered in gold from Egypt," he said, grabbing her piece off the board. "I'm sure you saw the sparkling stones set in the top. They are priceless."

As they continued to play and talk, Jasmine couldn't help noticing that Kav kept steering the conversation towards jewels or riches. She didn't think those things were very interesting, but Kav seemed to want to talk about nothing else. Despite her efforts to find out about the people he had met or the different sights he had seen, Kav kept talking about wealth.

"My biggest jewel is probably bigger than the biggest fig on this tree," he said. "It's a blue sapphire."

Jasmine smiled politely as she moved her horse-shaped figure across the board.

"Do you have any jewels that big?" Kav asked, moving his castle-shaped piece.

"Oh, I don't think so." Jasmine glanced up at the figs hanging from the tree's twisted branches. Her eyes narrowed as an idea came to her. "Do you want to know a secret about these figs?" she asked, determined to talk about something else.

Kav watched as Jasmine moved her chair closer to the tree and stood on it. She balanced on the tips of her toes and reached up to pluck two small ripe figs. She cradled

them in her hands and jumped down from the chair. "The smallest ones are the best," she said, offering him a fig. "They're the sweetest." She popped a fig into her mouth and then sat down to make her move.

"That may be true of figs," said Kav, eyeing the board. "But the larger the jewel, the better."

When Kav moved his horse-shaped figure away from his queen, Jasmine couldn't help smiling. She moved her castle piece across the board, capturing his queen.

Suddenly, Kav stopped talking. Seeing that Jasmine was winning, he focused on his next move.

They played silently for a few more minutes. Then, Kav knocked the board over with his knee, scattering the pieces to the ground. They both began to pick them up as Kav said, "I don't know how I did that."

"That's all right," said Jasmine. "I remember where all the pieces were. We can set it up the way it was and finish the game."

"No," Kav said, as he began putting the pieces back in the pouch. "I'm tired of chess. We should do something else."

Jasmine helped Kav tidy up, wondering if he had ended the game on purpose. She had been only a few moves away from taking his king and winning. But she pushed the thought out of her mind. She didn't want to believe her new friend would do something like that.

"Would you like to play hide-and-seek?" she asked, hoping to find something else they could do together.

Kav shrugged and walked off, carrying his game.

Jasmine sighed and followed him into the palace. She'd had no idea playing with someone could be so difficult!

Chapter 5
Trying to Have Fun

Jasmine convinced Kav to play hide-and-seek. She counted first while he hid. When she found him crouched behind one of the big flowerpots on the patio, he seemed a little annoyed. "Now it's my turn to seek," he said, and he quickly covered his eyes and began counting.

Jasmine ran off and soon found a good hiding spot underneath the patio stairs. But when Kav couldn't find her right away, he grew impatient. After only about a minute of searching, he announced that he didn't want to play anymore.

Jasmine came out of her hiding place and suggested they try to catch Rajah instead. It was fun to chase the speedy tiger around. They ran across the lawn and through the gardens. But Kav seemed angry when Jasmine caught the tiger before he did. "This is boring," he said. "And I think I have something in my shoe."

Jasmine and Rajah watched as Kav checked inside his shoe. "Are you okay?" she asked.

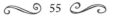

Kav nodded. "It was just some dirt," he said, shaking out his shoe.

"Do you want to play something different?" asked Jasmine, hopefully. She wished she knew a game that would be fun for both of them. Kav didn't seem to be enjoying himself at all. And trying to keep him happy wasn't much fun for Jasmine.

"No. It must be time to eat," said Kav. "And my feet hurt," he added, stomping off.

Jasmine wondered what she was doing wrong. Why was it so difficult to play with Kav?

Later on, when they all sat down to dinner, Kav barely said a word. After trying to talk to him a few times, Jasmine ended up sitting quietly throughout the meal as well. The Sultan and Gazsi chatted away the whole time. Neither of them seemed to notice the silence from the other side of the table.

Once their guests went off to bed, the Sultan invited Jasmine to the courtyard to have tea. "I want to tell you about the game," he whispered with a wink.

The two spoke for a long time under the stars. Jasmine enjoyed hearing all about the chess match, and the Sultan was happy to tell her every detail. He explained that the two men were playing very slowly, with lots

of conversation between moves. Surprisingly, they had each taken an equal number of the other's pieces.

"Now you tell me how it's going with Kav," said the Sultan. "Are you having fun?"

Jasmine forced a smile and lowered her head. "We played some games," she said. "He brought his own chess set, and we played that…" She trailed off, not sure how to answer her father's question. "Kav seems nice, but…"

The Sultan could tell his daughter was sad. "What is wrong, my dear?" he asked.

Jasmine told her father how Kav didn't want to finish any of the games they played and how he had stomped off. "Then he barely said a word during dinner," she added.

The Sultan nodded. "Yes… I thought you were both just tired. I'm sorry you aren't having fun."

"It's just that… well, I wonder what I'm doing wrong," Jasmine said with a sigh. "Maybe I don't know how to be a friend."

The Sultan frowned. "It sounds like Kav is the one who doesn't know how to be a friend."

"But he's travelled and met so many people. My only friend is a tiger." She glanced down at the tired cub curled round her feet and patted him on the head. "And we never care about who wins or loses," she added. She paused and looked up at her father with an idea. "Maybe I should let Kav win. Maybe he doesn't like to play unless he wins, so—"

The Sultan interrupted. "Jasmine, you cannot build a friendship by pretending to be someone you are not," he said. "I hope you would never lose a game on purpose or act like someone other than your true self to make someone like you."

Jasmine listened to her father's words and let them sink in. She knew in her heart that he was right. "So what should I do?" she asked, still wanting to be Kav's friend.

"It takes time for a friendship to grow,"

the Sultan said. "Some more than others. You should be patient." He leant towards her and put his hand on her arm. "But no matter what, you must always be yourself. Your beautiful, strong, kind, smart, Princess

Jasmine self." He lovingly brushed a piece of hair away from her face.

Jasmine thanked her father for his wise advice. "Maybe games aren't the best way to play with Kav," she said, thinking aloud. "I'll think of something else to try tomorrow."

"That's the spirit," the Sultan said. Then, they turned and walked arm in arm towards the palace. "Anyone would be fortunate to call you their friend. How fortunate I am to call you my daughter." He gave her a squeeze and a kiss goodnight.

Chapter 6
A New Strategy

The next morning, everyone had breakfast together on the high terrace. It was one of Jasmine's favourite spots, mostly because of the incredible view. Not only could they see the grounds from up there, but they could also see the kingdom of Agrabah beyond the palace walls.

Jasmine looked across the kingdom as she bit into a pastry, enjoying the sweet flavour of dates mixed with soft, warm bread. "That view makes me want to jump down there and see everything," she said.

"You have the spirit of an adventurer," said Gazsi with a smile. "Just like your father."

"Yes, I think you are right," agreed the Sultan.

Jasmine turned to Kav. "I think we should explore the grounds today," she said brightly. "Want to?"

Kav thought about it for a moment before muttering, "Sure."

"Wonderful," said the Sultan, looking proudly at his daughter. "Great idea."

Jasmine smiled as she took another bite of pastry. The day was off to a good start.

When everyone had finished breakfast, they headed back inside the palace. Gazsi and the Sultan told Kav and Jasmine to have fun and then hurried off, eager to get back to their chess game.

With Rajah at her heels, Jasmine led Kav outside and past the big fountain. "I'm so happy we're doing this," she said. "I've never explored the grounds with anyone but Rajah." She dipped her hand in the water, sending ripples across the surface.

They walked on the sprawling green lawn and Jasmine pointed at a hill. "There's a small grove on the other side," she said. "Let's go that way." Kav agreed and the two continued, heading towards the hill.

"I can't believe you've never been outside the palace walls," said Kav. "I've travelled the world, and you haven't seen anything but this." He held out his hand and swept it around, gesturing to the grounds.

"That's the rule," Jasmine said, sensing a tiny prick of anger in the pit of her stomach. She couldn't help feeling as if Kav had turned the conversation into his own kind of game – a game only he could win.

She took a deep breath. As she continued to walk, she thought about chess. In chess, it was important to think ahead. Jasmine had become better at guessing her opponent's moves before he made them. Perhaps she needed to think that way while spending time with Kav.

"I don't like the rule, though," Jasmine said. "So maybe one day I'll change it." As they crested a hill, she pointed out three large trees in a small valley below. "There's the grove." The trees were the same size and were huddled together like giants sharing a secret. They stretched towards the blue sky, both tall and skinny.

"Cypress trees," said Kav.

"Let's race to them!" Jasmine shouted without thinking. As the words came out of her mouth, she wished she could take them back. The last thing she wanted to do was to challenge Kav to a game. What if she won? She didn't want to send him stomping off again.

Kav nodded. "Okay, but let's roll down the hill."

Jasmine liked the sound of that. She had never rolled down a hill before and asked Kav to show her what to do. He was happy to teach her. Jasmine lay down on the ground and put her hands straight up above her head. Once she started to go, she began rolling faster and faster. Rajah happily ran alongside her as she picked up speed down the steep hill. She laughed as the world turned over and over again.

When she finally stopped at the bottom, she sat up, laughing so hard her stomach began to ache. Rajah pounced on her and covered her face with kisses.

Kav was waiting at the bottom. He was smiling, too!

"You look like your father," said Jasmine through her laughter. She noticed that Kav's nose bent towards his mouth like his father's

did when he was happy. "This is the first time I've seen you smile."

"That was a very good hill," said Kav, giggling with excitement.

"I loved it," said Jasmine. "Let's do it again!"

The two were unable to stop grinning as they ran up the hill. At the top, Jasmine knew what to do. She stretched out in the grass next to Kav and they set off rolling again, laughing the whole way down.

At the bottom, Jasmine sat up and felt as if the ground was moving. "The world is still spinning," she said. "I'm dizzy."

"Let's go sit in the shade," said Kav. He stood up and reached out his hand, offering to help her up.

Jasmine looked up at him and grabbed it. "Thank you," she said, a little surprised at his kind gesture.

The two walked over to the cypress trees. Jasmine watched as they swayed gently in the breeze. "They look like they're dancing," she said.

"Trees don't dance," said Kav. He looked at Jasmine and shrugged. "But I can see why you would say that." Then, he reached into his pocket and held out two small squares.

"These are sweets from India. Honey and pistachio. Would you like one?"

Jasmine nodded, and Kav handed her a sweet. She popped it in her mouth, closed her eyes and took a deep breath, savouring the moment. The honey softened and she got to the pistachio in the centre of the sweet. She crunched on it with her teeth and smiled, delighted by the salty flavour.

Jasmine looked up at the trees and remembered a story she had read, one she knew Kav would like. "Have you ever heard the story about the cypress trees that guarded treasure?" she asked.

Kav shook his head.

Jasmine explained that according to the story, the trees protected a king's gold. Anyone who tried to steal the treasure vanished. "It was the cypress trees that made the thieves disappear," she said. "The roots reached up, grabbed the thief and swallowed him. Then a sapling would grow."

"So the thieves turned into trees," Kav said.

Jasmine nodded and continued, "And soon a whole forest grew... protecting the gold forever."

"That's a good story," said Kav, looking

around. "I wonder if these trees are guarding treasure." Then, something caught his eye. "Look over there." He pointed towards a large cluster of boulders and rocks.

"What is it?" Jasmine asked.

"Over by the boulders," he said, walking towards them. "Do you see the space between them? It looks like they're blocking something."

Jasmine followed and, as they neared the boulders, she could see that Kav was right. Through the cracks was what appeared to be an endless space.

"Help me push these aside," said Kav, trying to roll a few of the large rocks out of the way. He and Jasmine moved them and revealed a shocking sight – a hole large enough to crawl through. It was a hidden entrance!

Chapter 7
An Exciting Discovery

The two peered into the hole, where they could see a rocky path leading down into darkness. Rajah sniffed around the entrance, inspecting it.

"I wonder what's down there," said Jasmine, excitedly. "It could be a secret passage."

"Maybe there are hidden treasures," said Kav.

They agreed to go inside and explore. Jasmine was thrilled by the prospect of a real adventure and squeezed through the opening. She turned to see Rajah standing still, nervously staring at her from the other side.

"Rajah," she cooed. "Come on, it's all right." She held up her hands, coaxing him in, and the little tiger cub cautiously crept through.

Kav followed behind Rajah. They had to crouch down to walk the steep, rocky path. Dusty rocks rolled around their feet, forcing them to slow their pace.

Once they got to the bottom of the path,

high dirt walls rose all around them and the space opened up, becoming large enough to stand in. "It's a tunnel!" said Jasmine, walking into it, mesmerised.

The two stood taking in the sight. The curved ceiling of the tunnel was jagged, as were the walls, with rocky ledges that jutted out from the sides.

"I wonder how long this has been here," said Jasmine, running her hand across one of the cold rocks sticking out of the wall.

"Could be thousands of years," said Kav, kicking up dust with his foot.

They walked round a curve and Jasmine

gasped as the light disappeared. She widened her eyes, straining to see.

"Do you want to turn round and go back?" Kav asked.

"No," Jasmine quickly responded. Even though she felt scared, her curiosity was stronger than her fear. She carefully placed one foot in front of the other and continued through the darkness.

"I bet there really are treasures down here," said Kav, slowly following her. "Great big ones!"

As the two walked quietly through the tunnel, Jasmine tried to picture a map of the palace in her mind to keep track of where they might be. She was certain that they hadn't left the grounds. It was so wonderfully strange to be walking beneath them!

Suddenly, a small flickering light cracked through the darkness ahead. It was a tiny lantern! Jasmine picked it up and used it to see their surroundings. "Who do you think this belongs to?" she whispered.

"It's ours now," Kav said. Then, he spotted something partially buried in the ground. "Bring the light over here!" Jasmine held the lantern as Kav dug through the dirt. He picked up a sharp, triangular white object.

"Could be an ancient animal's tooth," he whispered. "Probably worth a lot of money." He tucked it in his pocket and the two continued through the tunnel. It curved and snaked through the grounds, and whenever they reached what they thought would be the end, they found merely a tight bend. Each curve led to another stretch in the maze-like tunnel.

Soon, Jasmine noticed footprints in the dirt. "Look," she said, pointing. "I think there might be someone else down here."

Kav looked around. "If there is, they're probably looking for treasure, too. Let's just hope we find it first." His eyes ran up and down the walls and across the ground as they continued.

Jasmine held the light out in front of her. She took several more steps and heard a shuffling noise ahead. "What was that?" she whispered.

Kav shook his head. "I didn't hear anything."

"Footsteps," Jasmine said. "We aren't alone."

"I think you're just scared," said Kav.

Jasmine frowned. She knew she had heard something.

They walked farther through the tunnel, and when they turned another tight corner, Jasmine gasped. Someone *was* there, and he was standing right in front of them!

Chapter 8
The Mystery of the Tunnels

A boy stood frozen, staring at Jasmine and Kav with dark-brown eyes as round as saucers. His face and clothes were spotted with dirt, and he held a small lantern just like the one they had found.

"Hello," said Jasmine, smiling kindly at him.

The boy nodded and quietly responded, "Hello."

Kav glared at the boy, looking him up and down. "Who are you, and how did you get down here?" he asked boldly, stepping closer.

"My name is Babak," the boy said. "I work in the palace with my family. My father is Armand, servant to the Sultan."

As soon as he mentioned Armand, Jasmine could see the similarity to her father's loyal servant in his face.

Kav narrowed his eyes. "Do you know who this is?" he asked Babak, gesturing to Jasmine.

Babak glanced at Jasmine and shook his head.

"She is the princess," Kav said sharply. Then, he leant towards Jasmine and whispered, "He's either a fool or a liar – probably looking for treasure."

"Kav!" Jasmine said, shocked at how he was treating the boy. Babak quickly placed his lantern on the ground and knelt down, bowing his head.

"I'm sorry, Princess," Babak said, his voice shaking as he apologised. "I have never had the pleasure of seeing you... and I never would have expected to meet you here."

"Please stand up. You're too kind, but there's no need to bow," said Jasmine.

Babak stood cautiously. Jasmine asked him what he knew about the tunnel.

Babak shifted his feet uncomfortably. "It's actually a web of tunnels. They're used by the palace staff so that we can get around easily. They're shortcuts." He went on to explain that he liked to play in the tunnels. "I know my way around them pretty well," he added. "So I can usually get back before anyone even notices I'm missing." Babak smiled and then looked as if he was afraid he had said the wrong thing.

"And what are you doing down here now?" Kav asked.

"Well…" Babak hesitated. He admitted that he had been trying to learn how to play the ney, a flute-like musical instrument made of a hollow reed with holes across the side. "I'm not very good," he said. "I like to come down here to practise, where no one can hear me."

"Well, where is it, then?" demanded Kav, sounding sceptical. "Your ney."

"That's just it," said Babak. "I was practising yesterday and left it somewhere."

Babak explained that it was his grandfather's and he would never forgive himself if he lost it. "I have to find it and get back to work before anyone starts looking for me."

Kav pulled Jasmine aside. "We should go back to the palace immediately," he whispered.

"We should help him first," said Jasmine. "Maybe he wants to come play with us after he finds his ney."

Kav disagreed. "This whole encounter is improper," he said in a harsh whisper. "I'm sure your father would not be pleased that we are down here. And he most definitely wouldn't want you playing with a servant boy. What you are doing is wrong."

Jasmine looked at her feet. Her father had said she shouldn't play with anyone who wasn't royal. But he had also taught her to treat all people with respect, and the Sultan was always kind to the staff. Besides, she knew that helping Babak was the right thing to do, and she wasn't afraid to stand up for what she knew was right.

Jasmine faced Kav. Looking directly into his eyes, she said firmly, "I'm going to help Babak. And then after that I will go back to the palace."

"Fine." Kav turned his back to her. "I will return myself. I'll find my own way." He grabbed the lantern and headed off. "And I'll be sure to tell your father everything," he called as he disappeared round a corner.

Chapter 9
Jasmine's Rules

"Have you retraced your steps?" Jasmine asked.

"I thought I had," said Babak, nervously. "I'm pretty sure I left it on one of these high ledges." He gestured to the rocks jutting out of the wall. "I just can't remember where."

"Don't worry," said Jasmine. "We'll find your ney."

Babak became more relaxed as he and

Jasmine searched the tunnels together. Jasmine asked him how he had learnt to play the ney, and Babak explained that he was teaching himself. "I wanted to surprise my grandfather. Another reason why I've been practising down here," he said with a shy grin.

Jasmine suggested that Babak search one side of the wall while she and Rajah looked along the other. "That way we can save time," she said.

As they walked and searched, Jasmine told Babak about how she and Kav had spent the day exploring the grounds. She told him about rolling down the hill, about the cypress trees and about how they had stumbled upon the entrance to the tunnels.

"That's strange," said Babak. "I didn't know there was an entrance there, and I know these tunnels like the back of my hand. They must have been closed up a very long time ago." He warned Jasmine to be careful. "Some say there are snakes in the tunnels, all different kinds, even vipers with poison in their cheeks." He puffed out his cheeks, demonstrating.

"Have you ever seen any?" Jasmine asked.

"Only once," he said, explaining that it had been a very small black snake. "It slithered away before I could get a good look at it."

Jasmine and Babak chatted as they continued to search. The time passed quickly, and before long, Jasmine spotted the ney high up on a rocky ledge jutting out of the wall, just like Babak had thought.

Babak happily reached for the long, hollow reed and breathed a big sigh of relief. "Thank you, Princess," he said.

"You're welcome," she replied. "Will you play it for me?"

Babak was shy, but he could not deny her. He held the instrument up to his mouth, put it in place and began to play. At first, the instrument made a slight hissing sound. But then an airy melody began to rise above the hiss.

Jasmine smiled, watching his fingers moving over the holes in the hollow reed. She thought about Miss Leila, her father and Kav – they all agreed that she should not befriend people who weren't royal. But as Babak played, his eyes twinkling joyfully and his music filling the tunnel, Jasmine knew that the rule was unfair. *That's another rule I'll change one day,* she thought.

When Babak stopped playing, Jasmine clapped her hands, delighted. "That was truly wonderful!" she exclaimed. "Please play some more."

Babak began another song, playing as they headed towards the exit. The two had fun marching and dancing to the music. Even Rajah seemed to prance along, enjoying the tunes.

Then, a deep rumbling cut through the song, causing them to stop in their tracks.

They heard a crash, and then a panicked voice screamed, "Help!" Jasmine recognised the voice right away.

It was Kav! He must be in trouble!

Chapter 10
New Treasures

Jasmine and Babak rushed towards the sound of Kav's voice and found him buried up to his waist in a pile of dirt and rocks! The tunnel entrance behind him was blocked. Kav looked completely shocked as he explained that as he was climbing out of the tunnel, the ceiling collapsed. His face turned red as he strained to push himself up. "I—I can't move!" he cried.

"Don't worry! We're going to dig you out!" Jasmine exclaimed. She, Babak and Rajah immediately started digging, pushing away mounds of dirt and rocks.

Jasmine eyed the exit, now completely covered, and told Babak and Rajah to put the dirt behind Kav to try to avoid another collapse. Then, she asked Babak if he could lead them to another exit once they freed Kav.

"Yes," Babak said, nodding. "I can take you to one closer to the palace."

Kav was almost free from the rubble when suddenly his eyes went wide and he gasped. Jasmine and Babak turned to see a big brown snake coming up behind them!

"Nobody move," said Jasmine, reaching out and placing a firm hand on Rajah.

Kav, who was still stuck, started to panic as he watched the snake slowly slither towards him. "It's coming closer," he whispered, fearfully.

Jasmine had read about snakes with Miss Leila. She knew that they didn't like to go near people and would normally bite only if they felt threatened. "The worst thing we can do is panic," she said, calmly. "Stay very still and we'll all be fine."

Kav stared into Jasmine's eyes, listening

to her words and trying his hardest to remain calm. But the snake continued to come towards him, and he trembled with fear.

"Hold your breath," Jasmine said. She knew that if she gave Kav something else to focus on, it would help him stay still. "We'll all do it: one, two, three…" All three held their breath as they watched the snake curl through the dust and dirt. Finally, it made its way past Kav and disappeared into a small hole by the cave wall. They were safe.

They each breathed a huge sigh of relief and dug even faster to get through the remaining dirt and rubble as quickly as

possible. When Kav was finally free, he tried to get up, but his ankle gave out beneath him. He slipped and yelped in pain.

"My ankle!" he cried. "I must have twisted it when I fell."

Jasmine knew Kav wouldn't be able to walk back on his own. He stood perched on one foot as he looked down, feeling ashamed and helpless.

"We'll help you," said the princess.

Babak and Jasmine stood on either side of Kav. "Put your arms round us," Babak told him.

Kav lowered his head and glanced at Babak. "Thank you," he said sincerely, wrapping his arms round Babak's and Jasmine's shoulders.

Babak smiled and led the way as he and Jasmine slowly walked beside Kav, supporting him. When they reached the exit, Babak and Jasmine helped Kav out, and they all emerged above ground. The sun was starting to set, turning the sky bright pink streaked with gold. The palace grounds seemed to glow. The three stood for a moment enjoying the sight.

Kav turned to Jasmine and Babak and thanked them again. "I don't know what I would have done if you hadn't come to help me," he said. He took a deep breath before continuing. "And… I'm sorry. I wasn't being very nice. I shouldn't have walked off like that."

Jasmine and Babak both accepted Kav's apology and said, "You're welcome."

"I'm covered in dirt," Kav said, embarrassed. He brushed his hands against his trousers, trying to shake off the dust. Then, he reached into his pockets and looked up at Jasmine as he pulled out handfuls of rubble. "My treasure," he said, dropping the rocks on the ground. "I must have lost it in the fall."

Jasmine bent down and picked out three rocks from the pile. "Here's a new treasure. And there's one for each of us," she said, handing each boy a rock and taking one for herself. "Now we'll always have something to remind us of our great adventure together."

Babak grinned from ear to ear, touched by Jasmine's gesture.

Kav looked down at the dirty rock in his

hand and felt its rough edges with his fingers. "A jewel from the princess of Agrabah," he said with a smile. "Not exactly sparkling…"

"But beautiful and mysterious," Jasmine said.

Kav and Babak both thanked Jasmine and slipped the rocks into their pockets.

"Now we'd better get back," said Jasmine. "It's late." Kav put his arms round her and Babak again. The trio slowly made their way towards the palace, with Rajah following behind.

The Sultan and Gazsi were anxiously waiting in the palace courtyard. "Oh thank goodness," the Sultan said when Jasmine

appeared. He threw his arms round her and hugged her tightly.

"We were starting to get worried," Gazsi said.

"I was very worried," said the Sultan, finally releasing Jasmine from his hug. Gazsi and the Sultan looked down at Kav's foot as he held it gingerly off the ground.

Kav explained that he had fallen and twisted his ankle. "But Jasmine and Babak helped me," he added.

"Thank you both," said Gazsi, smiling at them gratefully.

The Sultan's eyes met Babak's. "Babak?" he said. "You are Armand's son, aren't you?"

"Yes," Babak whispered nervously, bowing his head. "And I'm sure he is looking for me," he added.

The Sultan thanked Babak for helping Jasmine and Kav, and then Jasmine prepared to say goodbye. "Good luck with the surprise," she whispered to her new friend as they parted.

The Sultan sighed with relief as he rubbed his head. "Let's go inside and sit down," he said. "Kav, we can have the healer look at your ankle right away. After, you can both tell us what happened. I have a feeling you have a lot to share."

Chapter 11
Adventures to Share

The doctor tended to Kav's ankle and informed them that it was sprained. With a little time, it would heal.

During dinner, Jasmine and Kav told their fathers about their exciting day. The men were relieved that their children were safe and seemed tickled that they had had an adventure of their own.

The next morning after breakfast,

Jasmine and the Sultan said goodbye to their guests. Kav looked at Jasmine with his jade-green eyes, as if he had something he wanted to say.

"Goodbye, Kav," said Jasmine.

Kav shifted his feet, still struggling to form the right words in his mind before saying them. "Jasmine," he said, then paused. Finally, he took a deep breath and continued, "Thank you." Then, he handed her a bag.

Jasmine peered into the bag and couldn't believe her eyes: it was his chess set. "But—"

"I want you to have it," said Kav. "For helping me. For being kind." He looked down at his feet. "I know I'm not always easy to get along with."

Jasmine was shocked by his gesture and his words. "Thank you, Kav," she said. "That is very generous."

Kav smiled, and his nose bent towards his mouth. "Maybe one day we'll play again," he said. "But I'll have to practise first."

"That would be lovely," said Jasmine.

As they parted, Kav held up his hand, waving the rock she had given him. "I will treasure it always," he said.

Jasmine and the Sultan watched as the horses carried the beautiful golden carriage away.

"I forgot to ask," said Jasmine, turning to her father eagerly. "Did you win your game?"

The Sultan nodded. "I did."

"What did you win?" she asked. "What was it that you bet?"

"Come," he said. "I will show you."

Jasmine followed the Sultan through the front door of the palace and into his office. She imagined her father and Gazsi betting mounds of gold, crowns or jewels. Her mind raced, wondering what the prize could be.

Finally, the Sultan reached into his desk and pulled out a small old box.

Jasmine gasped as she took in the sight

of it. It looked just like the one that her father had described in his story about him and Gazsi and the mysterious tower.

"Go ahead and open it," said the Sultan.

Jasmine slowly opened the box. She looked at the strange artifact inside. "The medallion!" she exclaimed.

The Sultan chuckled. "The medallion," he said.

Jasmine picked up the small piece of metal and felt its rough, scratched edges. It was spotted with colours – green, grey and copper – and had a misshapen hole cut out of the centre and a swirly design etched on its surface.

"That is what we always bet," said the Sultan. "The object of our favourite adventure together." He leant closer, whispering, "I'm glad I won it back!"

Jasmine smiled. "Me too." She gazed at the old medallion for another moment, flipping it over before giving it back to her father. Then, she reached into her pocket and pulled out her rock from the tunnel and showed it to him.

The Sultan examined it thoughtfully. "Looks like an ordinary rock." Before Jasmine could defend her souvenir, he added, "Isn't it wonderful? How something that appears ordinary can mean so much more?" He told her he was very happy she had something to help her remember her adventurous day. "It's beautiful. I am proud of you for being so brave and strong. You helped Kav without hesitation. You were a very good friend."

"Thank you, Father," Jasmine said, honoured by the compliment. It felt good to have learnt that she did know how to be a friend. She had even made two! "But Babak was also a good friend to Kav and me."

"He sounds like a fine boy. Armand must be proud of his son," the Sultan said, handing the rock back to Jasmine.

Jasmine clutched the jagged rock in her

hand and knew she would treasure the memories of the day and the friendships she had made forever. She loved her rock just as much as her father loved his medallion. It reminded her that friendships could be  found in the most unlikely places.

"Father, now that Kav is gone, I'll have no one to play with. But Babak lives nearby. We can play and never have to leave the palace grounds."

"Jasmine, my answer remains the same," the Sultan said sternly. "Though Babak is a nice boy, he is not royal." He turned away from Jasmine and headed towards his chambers.

But Jasmine wasn't finished. The Sultan had made his decision, but she knew it was the wrong one. She ran up to her father and faced him. "You've always taught me to treat everyone with kindness and respect. Why should it matter if a friend is royal or not? You even just stated that something ordinary can mean so much more," she said, now blocking her father. "Rules can be changed."

"Jasmine—" the Sultan began.

Jasmine had to think fast. She had to

convince her father while he was still in a good mood.

"I'll play you for it," she said with a sly smile.

The Sultan's face softened. "Oh, all right. If it means that much to you, I'll arrange a play date for you and Babak. But you must stay inside the palace gates, young lady."

"Thank you, Father!" Jasmine threw her arms round him and they embraced. She smiled, knowing she could find a whole new world within the vast palace grounds.